FOR OSCAR, PIPER, BO, AND SELAH
(WITH GRATITUDE FOR THEIR FATHER)
—N. D. W.

FOR MY DOG, ANN, WHO NINJA-SNEAKED
HER WAY INTO MY HEART
—J. J. H.

Text copyright © 2014 by N. D. Wilson
Cover art and interior illustrations copyright © 2014 by J. J. Harrison

Visit us on the Web! randomhouse.com/kids

Educators and librarians, for a variety of teaching tools,
visit us at RHTeachersLibrarians.com

Library of Congress Cataloging-in-Publication Data
Wilson, Nathan D.
Ninja boy goes to school. — First edition.
pages cm.
Summary: "A little boy explains what it's like to go to school—when you're a ninja." —Provided by publisher.
ISBN 978-0-375-86584-8 (trade) — ISBN 978-0-375-96584-5 (lib. bdg.) — ISBN 978-0-375-98179-1 (ebook)
[1. Ninja—Fiction. 2. Imagination—Fiction. 3. Schools—Fiction.] I. Harrison, J. J., illustrator. II. Title.
PZ7.W69744Ni 2014 [E]—dc23 2013033589

MANUFACTURED IN CHINA
10 9 8 7 6 5 4 3 2 1
First Edition

Book design by John Sazaklis

Random House Children's Books supports the First Amendment and celebrates the right to read.

NINJA BOY GOES TO SCHOOL

ELEMENTARY

by N. D. Wilson

illustrated by J. J. Harrison

Random House New York

It is hard being a ninja.

You must rise before the sun
and become one with the night.

You must possess the silence of a GHOST
(not the kind that wails and thumps) . . .

. . . the nimbleness of a MOUNTAIN GOAT
(but without the wool and horns) . . .

. . . the strength of a **GORILLA**

(but without the smell) . . .

. . . and the balance of a FLAMINGO
(but without looking silly).

It is hard being a ninja.
When you are a ninja, you will understand.

Ninjas must be one
with their surroundings.

A ninja must be still and patient,
like a deep-rooted tree . . .

. . . and strike with the *VIPER'S* speed when the time is right for disappearing.

A ninja's spirit is never caged.

A ninja leaps like a

GAZELLE

and floats like a
cherry blossom.

Ninjas must never give up.

Even when facing a strong enemy.

A ninja knows when to be silent.

PRINCIPAL PIE

In the face of injustice and hardship, a ninja's emotions are as smooth and still as a clear pond.

It is hard being a ninja.

When you are a ninja,
you will understand.

Don't forget, a ninja must learn to pretend that he is not really a ninja . . .

even though he is.